Billy on the Ball

by Paul Harrison

illustrated by Silvia Raga

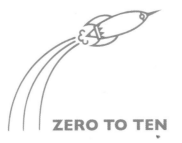

ZERO TO TEN

It's cup final day.

Billy's on the team.

The ground is full.

The game kicks off.

Billy heads the ball...

...and gets fouled.

Billy's on the ball again.

He shoots,

He's won the game!

He gets the trophy.

He lifts it high.

He wakes up!